Arion and the Dolphins

For Chi-Bin Chien,
in case he is ever young again

Text copyright © 1978 John L. Anderson
Illustrations copyright © 1978 Adrienne Adams

Library of Congress Cataloging in Publication Data
Anderson, John Lonzo, 1905-
Arion and the dolphins.
SUMMARY: Sailing home with a prize of gold won
in a contest, Arion faces death at the hands of the
crew who covet his treasure.
1. Arion — Legends. [1. Arion. 2. Folklore —
Greece] I. Adams, Adrienne. II. Title.
PZ8.1.A546Ar   813'.5'4 [398.2]   77-16564
ISBN 0-684-15128-6

1 3 5 7 9 11 13 15 17 19 YD/C 20 18 16 14 12 10 8 6 4 2

Printed in the United States of America

Arion and the Dolphins

based on an ancient Greek legend

by LONZO ANDERSON

illustrated by ADRIENNE ADAMS

Charles Scribner's Sons • New York

This boy was Arion.

He loved to play the lute and sing.

He made friends with the dolphins who lived in the sea. Naked he swam and played tag with them. For them he made his music day after day.

The dolphins dived and leaped in time with the music, and danced along the tops of the waves on the tips of their tails.

Arion lived in Greece, at Corinth, in the palace of the king, long, long ago.

The king told him of a musical contest. It was in Sicily, far away. The first prize was all the gold the winner could carry.

"Why, I can win that," said Arion.

Arion sailed to Sicily aboard a ship that had both oars and sail.

Every day he sat on deck practicing his music.

The oarsmen listened and sometimes forgot to row.

The sailors listened and forgot the sail.

And the dolphins followed the ship all the way, because Arion was there.

At Syracuse, a Greek city on the island of Sicily, Arion came to the musical fair.

He played and sang for a great crowd of people.

He won the first prize, all the gold he could possibly carry.

The ship set sail for home. Arion was on board with his gold.

The sky was crystal clear, blue, blue in the golden sunlight. The wind and the sea did everything to help the ship on its way, and the dolphins were there, escorting it home to Corinth.

The crew forgot about Arion's music and thought only of his gold.

Near the end of the homeward voyage, the seamen came to kill Arion for the gold.

There were too many of them. He could not fight them all.

"Let me sing one last song," he said quietly.

"That is reasonable," the captain said.

Arion stood in the bow of the ship.

He sang as he had never sung before. He played like an angel.

Even the most evil seamen listened with wonder. The birds flew down from the sky, and the creatures of the sea, from far and near, came close to hear this music.

And there beside the ship the dolphins swam.

Suddenly Arion leaped overboard.

The waves covered Arion. He clung to his lute. Down and down he sank, deep in the blue sea.

The dolphins were with him. One offered him a fin. She brought him to the surface before he could drown. He was so far from the ship that the seamen could not see him among the waves.

When the ship was out of sight, Arion climbed on the dolphin's back and rode her like a horse through the waves. The others swam along on all sides, chattering with joy.

The dolphins took Arion straight to his homeland, moving faster by far than the ship.

When the dolphins delivered him safe and sound on the beach, Arion thanked them with all his heart.

The dolphins leaped high in the air to show their pleasure.

In the distance stood the king's palace at Corinth. Arion traveled toward it.

Arion entered the palace, and the king came to
meet him.

When he heard what had happened, the king was
furious.

The ship reached the shore. The seamen came to the king to collect their pay.

"But where is Arion?" the king asked in anger.

"He did not return with us," the captain said.

Now Arion stepped out of hiding and faced the seamen.

They fell at his feet, begging for their lives.

The king roared at them, "You shall die! But you will never know when death may strike you, at any hour of the day or night, wherever you may be, whatever you may be doing. Now, bring Arion his gold!"

The seamen obeyed, then ran away in fear.

"Ho-ho-ho! Ha-ha-ha!" the king shouted, slapping his leg in delight.

Arion laughed along with him and said, "And they will never know that no one is going to harm them at all!"

Arion ran down to the seashore and sang to his friends, the dolphins, "Cooee, coohoo, ho-ho-ho! Cooay, cooah, ha-ha-ha!"

The dolphins listened and chattered and danced.

They seemed to be laughing too as Arion dived in for a swim with them.